Lost Hearts

Héca Riou

Lost Hearts

"All rights of reproduction, adaptation and translation, in whole or in part, are reserved for all countries. The author or publisher is the sole owner of the rights and responsible for the content of this book. The French Intellectual Property Code prohibits copies or reproductions for collective use. Any representation or reproduction in whole or in part by any process whatsoever, without the consent of the author or his successors or assigns, is unlawful and constitutes an infringement under Articles L.335-2 et seq. of the French Intellectual Property Code. "

This story is fictional and any resemblance to a real person or story is purely coincidental.

© 2023, Héca Riou, France
All rights reserved
ISBN : 978-2-3224-9964-9

Publisher: BoD – Books on Demand, info@bod.fr.

Printing: BoD – Books on Demand, In de Tarpen 42, Norderstedt (Germany)

Print on demand

Illustration : Picsart / Shutterstock

Legal deposit : August 2023

I hope my mother doesn't find out about this.

Sati

He was everything to me. After he took me in, my whole world revolved around him.

He taught me everything. Every trick, every technique, and above all, how to survive in a world made by men, for men. I'd grown up beside him, sometimes imagining him more as a father than a mentor, and he'd looked at me with the same benevolence that drove me to surpass myself every day so as never to cease impressing him.

I had become his greatest asset, his disciple, and so he took me everywhere with him, making me travel the country in search of all its hidden treasures, of which he was so avid. He cared for the unfortunates in our path, using the art of medicine to perfection, as well as that of persuasion, offering us ever more opportunities.

I had entrusted him with my life, which had so little value until I crossed his path, me, the nameless orphan, just good at stealing grain from merchants' pockets, with a hope blinded by the legend he represented. He intimidated me, no less than he fascinated me. He was my tutor, my role model, and had graced me with his indelible mark on the back of my neck, as proof that my trust in him was reciprocated.

But from one day to the next... I was nothing.

He'd gone, without a word, leaving me alone and unconscious in the middle of the desert, probably in the hope that I wouldn't survive.

Had I finally let him down? Was I too weak for his taste? Or had he simply lost interest in me over time?

All I could remember was the sweltering heat as I awoke, lulled by the lascivious march of the camel on which my "saviors" carried me, and the throbbing pain in my heart as I realised that the man for whom I had been willing to sacrifice everything had finally abandoned me.

I was Sati, a brilliant pupil of the healer Shaa-em-uas, destined for a great future in the court of the greatest in the land. Now I was just Sati. Nameless, and former apprentice to one of Egypt's now greatest criminals.

And that, I can tell you, on a CV, wasn't looking too good.

It took them months, between preventive detention and harsh interrogations, before determining that I was not a danger. And "worse" still, that I could give them little information about my mentor on the run, however violent their tortures might have been.

But all those days of suffering, without seeing the light of day, and without knowing when the next crust of bread would come along to feed me, were nothing compared to the emptiness I felt inside, lost in memories that wouldn't come back, appalled to discover that the man I'd admired so much had nothing in common with the one I was now being described as, and devastated at the idea of no longer having a single goal in front of me.

Or maybe one.

To see the bottom of that infamous jug of beer, which I was sipping quietly, sitting on the heights of Thebes.

Alcohol had become my best ally, since I'd been allowed to resume a "normal" life. I more than regularly drowned my failing memory in a jar, and when I finally crossed that holy boundary between reality and intoxication, I was fine. So fine...

I was just about to reach that sweet moment, when a weary voice, yet so sexy to my ears, pulled me prematurely from the intoxicating flavour of "one sip too many".

— I didn't think the place was already taken," apologised the man responsible for my incipient annoyance.
— I didn't know it was assigned to you, Amon," I retorted, in a scathing tone, forgetting any form of decorum demanded by my meager rank.
— That's not what I said," stressed the dark-haired man with an annoyed sigh, but not without sitting down beside me.
— Do you really intend to stay here and spoil my moment of personal happiness? I'm off duty here, in case you've missed it.
— Making a fool of yourself again? Don't expect me to take you home this time. And do I really need to wait until you're on duty to talk to you?

Well, at least I know how I got into bed last time... and probably all the times before. It's true that of all my customers, he was the only one who hadn't even looked at me. Yet he paid the keeper of the brothel to which I'd been relegated after my release dearly, just to pull up a chair and talk to me about various things, or read me entire papyri of stories he said he'd written. It was strange, but at the same time, how could I complain, since he was giving me a bit of peace and quiet in an environment where they didn't hesitate to overexploit you?

- Did you come all this way to lecture me?

Silence. He was once again immersed in one of his damn parchments. Where was I? Ah yes, my *heneqet*!
As the last drop rolled down my throat, a new sigh spoiled the flavour of this final moment.

— What now?" I breathed, deeply annoyed.
— You really should stop this bullshit.
— I don't see what it's got to do with you. I'm fine with it as it is," I grumbled involuntarily, under the effect of the alcohol that was fogging my brain less than I'd hoped.
— You're right, it's none of my business. But for your information, your reputation goes far beyond the walls of Thebes.
— And it's not as if I've got anything to make it better.

With that in mind, I stood up, wobbling as I caught myself on a block to keep my balance. Discerning a movement from Amon's side, I caught myself smiling. Beneath his air of indifference, I knew he was ready to catch me if I fell. He was like that. Distant and benevolent at the same time. Sometimes he pretended not to care, with his air of a dreamy storyteller, living in the opulence of high society, but the truth was that he couldn't bear the idea of seeing anyone hurt, no matter how low-born the person might be.

I then let myself slide up to his face, frozen in a grimace after being caught wanting to play the hero once again, strutting around in a balance that was more than precarious given the intoxication that continued to win me over, every second more and more.

— Ask me out.

I giggled at my foolishness, half-aware of the consequences such simple words could have. He had the power to send me back to the place I'd struggled so hard to get out of, and frankly, I didn't care; that fate seemed preferable to the one that would have sent me spinning through perverted hands in a building almost as unsanitary as the prison itself.

At last, he lifted his golden eyes, in a gaze that persisted in wanting to be inexpressive.

— Sati, I could smell your breath all the way across town. You're drunk. Go home.

I grumbled at the umpteenth dodge he offered me. This man remained a mystery, impervious to my every charm. He had even become a personal challenge. No one ever resisted me, or at least I never had to make the slightest effort to get a man into bed. They even paid for it. And while I did my best to remain detached, treating him as I would any of my customers, I couldn't help but be intrigued, even amused, and each of our verbal jousts made me feel alive, if only for a moment. I felt close to him, without really being close. We each lived with our own torments, and each decompressed in a more or less honourable way, which surely explained why we understood each other so easily.

— I propose a pact.

I stopped all of a sudden, without turning around, but he knew that I was all ears to hear what he had to say.

— Stop drinking, and I'll invite you in.

He was consciously arousing my defiant instincts. I loved to gamble, and he knew it, just as he knew how much I hated losing, or even declining a bet. My pride, or my heneqet. I smiled at the thought, determined to tease him:

— Is the reward really worth it?
— I can guarantee you won't be disappointed.

That's all I needed. I raised a hand in agreement as I descended the stairs without a glance at him. Pride. Sorry, heneqet.

Amon

I watched her leave with her nonchalant, unladylike gait, before savouring the quietude of my newfound place. Because, whatever she said, yes, it was MY place.

I plunged back into my reading, still unable to concentrate. How annoying that girl could be! So noisy and undisciplined, that even when she was gone, she prevented you from aspiring to the rest you so coveted.

I sighed as I rolled up my papyrus, resigned, and leaned my head against the cool wall, eyes closed. What was I thinking, challenging her like that? It was none of my business, after all. But to see her make such a spectacle of herself was no longer an option. She doesn't behave like a woman, even one of her rank. And if only that were her only fault. On top of that, she had to behave as if the whole of Thebes - or even Egypt - were at her feet. The entire male population of Thebes, to be exact. And the worst of it was that this was practically the case... At the same time, you couldn't blame anyone for not being insensitive to her... charms. Especially as she wasn't exactly at pains to conceal them.

I shook my head as my mind drifted. Get a grip Amon, it was only a silly challenge, and there's really little chance of her winning it.

Eventually, I made my way down to the town cemetery. How many of my friends were there? 5? 10? 30? I'd finally stopped counting. I'd long since given up the spear for the pen, wallowing in my new life of solitude, telling their tales, which continued to chill my blood, while entertaining my compatriots.

Don't get attached.

This had become my watchword ever since I had felt the heart of the woman promised to me extinguish beneath my fingers. Not to suffer any more, but above all because all the people who had had the misfortune to cross my path a little too closely were no longer of this world.

My father, my brothers, my friends... and her.

They were all gone, while I remained here, blindly devoting my life to continuing to bring my loved ones to life through stories I altered as I pleased, mostly omitting details that might have damaged their reputations. If we'd known peace earlier, my brothers would still be out there teasing the beautiful women of Thebes, and my father would never have sought to join them in a desperate gesture, abandoning me for fear of not being able to protect myself any more than they could, nor would I have had to watch my comrades-in-arms, my friends, collapse in a mixture of sand and blood, nor would I have lost my fiancée, the person I loved more than anything else in the world, in a kidnapping that only led us to pay this heavy price.

I was the only one responsible for this massacre, and yet I came out of it as a hero, ashamed and adored. But I had nothing left, and in a way, that was just as well. No ties, no problems.

At last, I climbed up onto my pedestal, facing my insatiable oratory, and once again told those stories whose truth I could no longer disentangle from falsehood. Their eyes, filled with compassion and pride, were in total contradiction with the weight that gripped my chest, but it was a small price to pay next to the guilt I could never atone for.

Sati

Several days had already passed, and I'd held out so far, despite the temptation after each end of shift, which repulsed me more than I'd imagined. Amon had better keep his word, there were things I hoped to forget, and if I couldn't get near a jar, he'd have to find another way! But difficult as it was, he was right. I was drinking too much, and had been for too long, my body had been reminding me of this ever since the first day of his bloody bet: the night sweats, the trembling, the constant desire to quench this endless thirst... All I had left was my pride, the only weapon I had left to resist, there was no way I was going to lose to this idiot! Now that I thought about it, he hadn't even told me how long I had to hold out like this... What a bastard!

In the distance, I noticed two men beckoning me to join them on the terrace, where they were enjoying a cool mug after a long day on guard duty. They were no strangers to me, of course, as it was not uncommon for the landlady to call on them to dislodge those who forgot that "her girls" only belonged to them for as long as they had paid, and that after all this time spent under the roof of our joint, we were now bound by a friendly relationship, with the hope of advantages that we were of course not allowed to concede to them.

Let's pretend I didn't see them. There was no need to make things difficult for myself, and besides, I didn't owe them anything. I was going to walk right past. At least, that's what I thought, when a large arm suddenly encircled my shoulders.

— So what, Sati! Aren't you joining us tonight? It's the first time I've seen you turn down an invitation!" bellowed the voice of Set, the man in charge of the cohort charged with protecting the neighbourhood, and without doubt the one who would be the most attractive, if he weren't scarred all over his face and half one-eyed.

Crap.

I'd have tried to come up with some lame excuse to get out of this hellish mess, but what could I say? They'd never take me seriously if I refused a free drink. All I had to do was smile and keep my hands on my knees. But as I sat down beside them, my opposite number's still half-full glass was already giving me the eye.

Just keep your hands under the table, there's no point in ruining all your efforts now.

The men laughed at their jokes, which I couldn't hear, and others soon joined in, like an old habit. Set's heavy hand tightened again on my shoulder, his arm encircling my neck, and he pressed me against him without the slightest delicacy, appropriating my presence without consent, practically making me climb onto his lap. Why the hell was he always so clingy?

But my attention was soon turned back to the glasses clinking under my nose, releasing a few fine droplets of the nectar my whole body was calling for. The conversations buzzed with the powerful voices of the guards, some of whom were already close to intoxication, but I didn't understand their content, too absorbed in my contemplation. I could feel a drop beading on my forehead; my mouth, on the contrary, was as dry as the air saturated by the ambient furnace of this late evening. I was thirsty, so thirsty... Just a drop, a sip... Amon wouldn't know!

My hand was only a few millimetres away from my coveted bliss, when a deep, irritated voice, which I had hoped never to hear at that moment, snapped me out of my obsession, as abruptly as my shame invaded me at the same instant:

— What are you playing at?!
— Amon! My brother! You've finally decided to come out of your hole! Come and have a drink with us!" invited Ao, the youngest of the guards, oblivious to the storyteller's obvious bad mood.
— What's the matter with you? Didn't your audience live up to your ambitions?" Set glared at him, squeezing me even more possessively.

I was suffocating, and nothing seemed to loosen his grip.

— Let her go, she doesn't belong with you.

Amon's order, so curtly pronounced, brought a stony silence to the regiment. He wasn't one to pick quarrels, and it was a mixture of curiosity and excitement that gripped the men, eager to see if they would come to blows. Set's hands, however, would have none of it. Stunned by this turn of events, I was left speechless, letting my skin react for me in an irrepressible shudder as he brushed it along the fabric covering my chest. Amon didn't flinch, although I'd swear his angular jaw was much more contracted than usual. Was he angry with me? I hadn't given in to temptation... at least not completely.

— What do you mean, nothing to do with us? Sati is our friend! What's got into you all of a sudden?" interrupted Ao, clearly no longer understanding what was going on.
— A friend you keep pushing to drink, knowing full well she'll either make a fool of herself again, or end up in I don't know who's bed.

Did I have to remind him that this was what allowed me to have a roof over my head, and enough to feed myself? But despite his icy tone, his last words resonated with me in a way that was as hurtful as it was worried. It wasn't so much what he was insinuating as what he feared — and he'd already admitted it to me, or rather reproached me, once or twice when he took me home — it was that one day I'd come across the "wrong one". Many girls had already disappeared without the slightest explanation, and above all, without anyone caring. And it was true that I often woke up in unfamiliar places, usually with a man by my side and a painful blackout in my skull. But that was my life, and there was nothing wrong with doing yourself good, was there? What did he care about?

The young guard said nothing more, and realising his "mistake", he immediately moved his glass discreetly away from me, his complexion pallid, just tinged with red at the top of his cheeks. Thank you, Amon. Now my "friends" are going to think I'm a drunk. At the same time... How many times had they come to warn him, only for him to come and talk some sense into me? Come to think of it, Amon was always there, although he wasn't really. He never drank with us or even spent a minute chatting. And yet, when I couldn't think for myself, he'd appear as if by magic. Growling, grumbling, criticising my behaviour, while carelessly carrying me on his back, strategically plucking me from the lair of one of my one-night stands a little too attached to me, or keeping watch outside my door while I bitterly regretted my excesses. He was always the one to call when I became unmanageable.

— She's an adult, she's entitled to decide for herself how she wants to enjoy her life. We're not all like you, aspiring to the life of a hermit.

Set... The one who never despaired that his bed would be the next one I stopped by. I knew he was madly in love, but I wasn't into sentimentality. I'd run away as soon as the word "love" came into my life, never allowing such problems to arise. I could no longer... No longer offer my trust... No longer depend on someone in this way, and risk being broken again if I had the misfortune to let my guard down.

Amon was about to retort again, but I passed him by finally speaking up:

— He's right, Set. I've decided to stop heneqet.

Amon's dark look, which smacked of deceit, prompted me to add:

— And any kind of alcohol, for that matter.

Set and the others immediately broke into laughter, and the looks of incomprehension from the more modest didn't really help me feel at ease with my nascent sobriety.

— I don't see what's so funny," growled Amon, who was decidedly too interested in what they thought of me.
— Sati probably agreed to this for your benefit!

Set! The traitor...

— It's amazing to see you paying attention to someone, and obviously your attention is all she's looking for! But it won't last three days, so we've got nothing to worry about! Sati's never been much for commitments," Set continued, as if he could claim to know me by heart, taking a big sip of his drink with the air of taunting me.

I disengaged myself from his grip, my eyebrows and nose wrinkling in annoyance at being mocked like that, but once again I didn't have time to defend myself on my own, as Amon and his detached air came to my rescue once more:

— How much, Sati?

He flatly ignored my suitor's revelations, and I immediately understood that he was trying to find out how many days had passed since the bet began.

— Seven...

— Tonight, at my place," he concluded, with an air strangely heavy with innuendo, as he was already walking away.

— You and the insensitive Amon Donkor?" teased Ao, a smirk on his face, as Set gulped down his mug in one gulp, far too upset now to get a word in edgewise.

Amon had it all planned, I was sure. It would be a simple, unpretentious dinner, but he couldn't help but make me uncomfortable in the process. At least it would cool Set down for a while. I took the opportunity to leave the tavern, the source of all my temptations, under the stunned gaze of the boys, who still didn't seem to come back from my new resolutions. I proudly gave them my best smile and a quick wave, before it occurred to Set to return to the fray and counter Amon.

The evening arrived much more quickly than I had anticipated, having spent hours shuffling my wardrobe in search of a suitable outfit. It has to be said that the many clothes I was gifted were more often fantasy than real. But this time, I wanted to be more elegant than sexy, taking up the challenge of making him, who wasn't interested in anyone, fall in love with me. And I knew from experience that the sight of a plunging neckline on my chest was not enough to make his heart skip a beat, since he'd never even brought his palm close to my flesh.

In the end, however, I opted for an ecru drape, which I tied around the nape of my neck, before letting it fall broadly over my chest, concealing it only slightly more than usual, while leaving my back bare down to my lower loins. The fabric fell to my ankles, leaving a glimpse of one of my legs only through a slit running up my thigh, provided my steps were long enough to move it aside. I loved fine finery, and took advantage of this unusual outing to tie belts and necklaces, adorn my arms with charms I'd found on the market, and adorn my hair with a few gilded accents, mixing my own finds with a few offerings I'd been able to appreciate. I wanted to be seductive, but above all, true to myself. I wanted Amon to see me as I was, and not as the sex toy I'd become by force of circumstance. After all, he seemed to enjoy my conversation more than my body, judging by his chaste visits. With a final glance in the mirror, after carefully combing my long ebony hair into a long braid falling down my spine, I worried that I'd overdone it. Or maybe not enough? Damn it, Sati, what exactly do you expect from this evening?! It was only a dinner party.

I finally took off my tiara to comfort myself in the idea of remaining as natural as possible, for some reason unknown to me, even though I was accustomed to exaggerating all the qualities nature had given me, in spite of the life it had offered me. And once I'd slipped on my sandals, I hurried towards the exit under the disillusioned gaze of my roommates and the lady of the house, barely recognizing me and probably wondering what I was doing in this get-up. But I had no desire to share any confidences on the subject, making Amon the object of a whole new secret garden. What's more, I was already late, but I'd learned long ago to make myself languish!

I opened the door with a dancing step, barely holding back all the joy I was feeling, a silly, unexplained smile stuck to my lips, before immediately freezing, red in the cheeks:

— What?!
— I've changed my mind," Amon replied, guessing my surprise as he leaned against the stoop's railing. I thought this was a chance to do something out of the ordinary for once.

It couldn't be said that this lessened my astonishment, quite the contrary. That he invited me was one thing, but that he should take such initiatives, at the risk of being seen by everyone in my company... If I'd expected it! I didn't miss his gaze, however, which was already wandering over me, seemingly studying the outfit I'd taken so much care to select.

— Do you like it?" I mocked lightly, masking all the flattery it inspired in me.

My efforts hadn't been in vain, it was the first time I'd caught him ogling me like that! But I certainly wasn't going to claim victory just yet!

— It's... different.
— You, on the other hand, didn't bother too much," I pointed out, ignoring his usual dodge, while pointing to his simple brown pants and immaculate white sweater, reminding him that we were definitely not in the same milieu.
— Comfortable," explained the storyteller, as his eye made what seemed to me to be a stop on my concealed chest, before returning to my face, sowing doubt in my trained mind as to the true reason for this adjective.
— So, finally... What do you suggest?" I deliberately used my most sensual voice, just to test him a little more.

Amon

God, that girl drove me crazy. She wasn't very tall, but her slender legs, barely covered as she leaned against the doorframe, and that voice that would make the holiest of men's heads spin, would have been enough to make me cut the evening short and go straight to her, even if it meant paying the price if I didn't take it upon myself to resist. That wasn't how I expected to get to her, not after spending so much time trying to make her understand that she wasn't just a brothel girl to me, a banal plaything in the hands of a man, an object whose favours you pay dearly for... I was foolishly getting carried away with the idea, all the money in the world wasn't enough to tear her away from this environment where I couldn't bear to see her. But what did I expect anyway? It was just an ordinary evening with friends, I shouldn't even be looking at her like that, I didn't want to look like one of those idiots who were always after her.

— Amon?

Her voice had changed this time, more worried, while I had lost myself in my thoughts. I lifted my eyes to hers, a green with a fine sprinkling of hazel, shining between her hair as dark as night, which she had let fall in a braided cascade down her back. She was so beautiful, radiant even in the half-light, fully deserving of the name 'Daughter of Ra'. Damn… I was just like *them*. Please don't repeat my name... Sati.

— Hm?

For Gods' sake, pull yourself together, man! Cat got your tongue?!

— I was asking you where you wanted to go... But if you're too tired to go out, we can postpone it for another time, you know.

She was worried... She who was always so casual was for once letting her feelings show. I could even discern a hint of disappointment at the idea of cancelling this evening. Did she really hope so? But it was out of the question. If she only knew how many times I wanted to propose to her... How many times I felt like an idiot when I saw her clinging to someone else's arm. But how could I admit it? We're not from the same world... And it went against our philosophy of life. The same one that made us understand each other so well.

— Follow me," I said in my constantly indifferent tone, which I was forcing more and more.

The flash of disappointment immediately turned into a luminous smile, and she took hold of my arm as if it were the most natural thing in the world. I would have pulled away to keep the distance between me and her, but her new-found good humour prevented me. She was sunny, so lively and enthusiastic that it was contagious. My heart, usually so cold, was immediately surrounded by a warmth that I had been unconsciously missing.

Nonetheless, I sighed for the sake of it, as I led her to the place that seemed to me the most in keeping with her personality: a festival celebrating the beautiful days to come. A festival with a thousand and one illuminations, where life was in full swing at the stalls run by the people of Thebes.

— Do you know that I love you?

I was startled by this brutal admission, not expecting such a declaration straight away, even from someone as impulsive as Sati. I was about to turn to her, ready to hurl back a retort full of innuendo that would confuse her even more, reminding me of what Set had said to me this afternoon, but I quickly thought better of it.

I must be dreaming...

She turned towards me, her arms laden with pastries made from honey and date paste, which she had snatched from the first stall we came across. She looked at them with such love and devotion that I could almost feel a pang of jealousy creeping into some dark corner of my heart.

Once again, I was behaving like a fool, imagining things that wouldn't happen. You don't talk about love with Sati, *never*.

She delicately placed one of the biscuits between her lips, the sweet taste of which I could guess would probably be left there as she passed. Damn it, Sati, you're not doing anything to help me...

I heard her chuckle, ignoring my borderline obscene thoughts, and her hand slipped into mine, pulling me without warning towards a games stall.

— Tug-of-war?" I wondered.
— At last we'll be able to see which of us is stronger! she sang, obviously far too sure of herself.

Did she think that because of my profession I only know how to do things with my mind? She seemed to have forgotten that underneath that outfit still hides a former soldier. But like her, I never turn down a challenge, and as we settled down face to face, each supported by other competitors, determined to restore the balance between us by unbalancing the numbers in her favour — not without annoying me at the same time to see her still being courted — she added in that damn voice so seductive to spike the bet:

— If I win, you can take me dancing there!
— I don't dance," I reminded her.
— In that case, you'd better not lose.
— What's in it for me?" I deliberately ignored this little provocation.
— I'll do anything you want.

Her voice, heavy with innuendo, finally made my cheeks turn red, while in my head, a thousand ideas, each more unmentionable than the last, were emerging. I was lucky she couldn't see it with the night already fallen and so little light.

— Ladies' honour," I simply grumbled, trying not to let on, as she grabbed the rope and pulled it towards her, staring at me with her big, fierce eyes.

Out of sheer pride, and even though it would take a lot more to make her move me even one iota, I didn't look away from her, ready to retaliate, implacable, while taking care not to hurt her in spite of everything.

Sati

I couldn't help drowning in the gold of his gaze, shining with defiance, or something else I didn't know, making me shiver despite the heat of that first summer night. When was the last time I felt myself vibrate with such intensity? The thought immediately brought me back to my old life, my hectic travels with Master Shaa-em-uas, his discoveries, ever more eager, ever more dark...

— Are you chickening out?" Amon challenged me, pulling me out of the nostalgia that was overtaking me.
— You're dreaming, darling!

I took advantage of the confusion I'd caused in his mind by using that nickname unintentionally, to pull the rope sharply towards me, sounding the death knell for the start of a frantic battle between Amon and his few acolytes, and my own, indecently unfair team. No matter! He wanted to play, and I'm going to win, even without the honours! Facing me, he didn't let himself be outdone so easily, contracting his muscles so intensely that I was finally able to make out much more clearly what was so difficult to hide in his baggy clothes.

— You'll end up slipping on your own spit," the cheeky man taunts me.

He may have hidden all his treasures, but he was still a narcissist! But at the same time, who could possibly dissuade him from having been blessed by Hator herself! My team-mates were doing their utmost to continue this idiotic game, drawing the bugger towards me, without him offering the slightest resistance. Time seemed to have stopped in a strange way, with no more spikes coming to tease us, just his pupils ablaze and his body so hot from the effort he had put in that his heat was reaching me despite the few centimetres that still separated us. I cursed my heart for stirring for this man whose eyes I couldn't take my eyes off. I hated myself for wanting him so much, because deep down, I could feel it, I was attracted to him. Not for one evening, not for one night. I wanted to discover him in his entirety, to know every one of his secrets, to tame his flaws, and above all... to feel his protruding arms around my body. How could I admit that I loved his conversation, even though he could talk for hours. That I liked even more his visceral, unconscious need to care about me. He didn't treat me the way other people did, and that's probably why everything was so confused in my fragile mind.

Don't get attached.

This wasn't the time to spoil everything, the evening was only just beginning and I hadn't yet given him the exquisite taste of my victory.

— It looks like you owe me a dance," I quipped a few millimetres from his face.

— You cheated," he refused, flicking me on the forehead and forcing me to take a step back.

No, but what a bad player! I followed him with a burst of laughter as he left the scene of his defeat far too quickly, and once again grabbed his large hand, which seemed made to fit mine, determined to get him into the area he was obviously trying to escape from. Whatever he said, I deserved my reward! I'd kept his bloody bet for seven days!

Without further ado, I slipped between the passers-by who were already dancing in the main square, to the rhythm of percussion and flutes. As I suspected, Amon persisted in staying in the background, but I hadn't said my last word yet. I knew him to be reserved and discreet, and despite his talents as an orator, he didn't really like making a spectacle of himself. But I never forgot that he could often surprise me, be playful and mischievous, and above all, that he had promised me an unforgettable evening!

I began to sway lasciviously to the rhythm of the music, which naturally carried me along, swaying my hips from side to side as I moved my hands above my head. Forgetting my daily routine for a moment, I played with my sensuality and glanced at him from time to time, noting with satisfaction that even though he was sitting a few metres away, he wasn't missing a moment of the show I was putting on for him. His eyes were unconsciously detailing my generous curves as they moved in the light of the braziers, in the midst of a group that he didn't even seem to notice any more. I was having fun concentrating all his attention, and I certainly didn't intend to leave it at that. Testing his limits, I let one man, then two, approach me, pretending to dance with them, since Mister Donkor had decided to abandon me on this dance floor. Unsurprisingly, they didn't waste any time, coming dangerously close, before placing their hands all too quickly on my uncovered loins. Their bodies rubbed insidiously against mine, letting me guess that their expectations went far beyond a simple dance. I lost sight of Amon very quickly, but I knew that he would keep me preciously in his field of vision, counting on a potential jealousy to finally incite him to join me.

I felt my hair pulled back, then the cool air on the back of my neck before the pain of a bite I hadn't anticipated. A startled sigh escaped me as I tried to subtly extricate myself from the grip of these men who were now intent on marking their territory. I had no intention of ending up in a stranger's bed tonight, least of all when I was in my right mind for once! They weren't exactly on board with the idea, but fortunately my plan finally seemed to work, as I soon found myself drawn against a body with a much more familiar smell.

— You took your time." I reproached my "saviour", without hiding the smile of satisfaction that was growing on my face.

Amon

— Idiot...

I whispered this simple word to her, holding her close to me as I passed my hand over her waist, under the aggressive gaze of her previous partners, which I returned without the slightest hesitation, urging them to flee immediately. Did she always have to get herself into this kind of situation to get my attention?

I sighed in annoyance, hating the bubbling feeling that had come over me as I watched these men try to possess her before my eyes, and continued to make her dance. She had finally won, and was glowing proudly in my hands. My heart softened at this, missing a beat as I spun her around, before bringing her and her warm smile back against me. Our movements were so natural and fluid that I forgot my notorious incompetence in this art that I had never practised, unlike her, who was so exquisite to admire.

Not getting attached.

She rested her head against my chest when the music changed to something softer. My hyperactive ray of sunshine was suddenly transformed into a gentle, fragile woman. She had so many different faces, and if for most of us she was this overexcited, always cheerful girl, I knew that with me she didn't play any roles, letting her emotions speak with modesty, as they came to her. We'd always been so close, without really being close at the same time, going through things separately, but always looking out for each other in our own way. It was now that I realised just how close we were, and how far from 'new' we were. She had listened to me for hours on end without ever cutting me off, and although I was paying for it, she never made me feel any lack of interest in my stories. If there were times when I doubted her honesty, I wondered just as much who could be capable of faking it without so much as a yawn for so long?

Lost in my thoughts, I finally put my chin in her hair, immediately becoming intoxicated by her scent of jasmine, mixed with something else I'd never been able to discern, but which made her even more unique. Time seemed to stand still again, it seemed to be a habit with her, and we continued to move slowly against each other, without a word, until the last note faded into the night.

She gently pulled away from my embrace, her cheeks slightly tinted red, and stood still, facing me, as the crowd dispersed and the torches gave off nothing but a cloud of smoke, plunging us into a darkness barely disturbed by the twinkling of the starry sky above our heads.

— I've had a lovely evening, Amon. I really did.

His confession broke the silence that surrounded us, announcing the end of this daydream. I wanted to tell her that I didn't want it to end yet, that I felt so good with her, more alive than ever, forgetting even the scars of my past. I was ready to break all those solid convictions I'd imposed on myself, for one more look, for a caress, or maybe a kiss. But I couldn't. I couldn't bring myself to risk losing her too, as if getting attached would automatically mean her death, or maybe worse. And Sati was doing the same anyway, running away from the idea of feeling anything for anyone, at the risk of getting her wings burnt off again.

— I'll take you home," I said instead, resigned.

She agreed immediately, taking hold of my arm again. I didn't know her to be so tactile, but I was getting the hang of it all too quickly. Would she still be the same tomorrow? I probably wouldn't have the slightest reason to worry about it, tomorrow would be a new day, and the timeless bubble we'd exchanged would be no more than a vague memory, before each of us went back to our own lives.

It was in this pensive silence that I walked her to the back of the establishment that housed her, reminding myself how different our lives were. She was already climbing the steps of the dilapidated staircase overlooking the dark street, out of sight, and I mechanically followed her, blurting out her name without even knowing what I wanted to say:

— Sati...

Sati

I turned around, not expecting to come face to face with him straight away. He towered over me, forcing me to lift my head, waiting for him to say goodbye, or goodnight, or whatever banality would conclude this evening once and for all.

But he said nothing, motionless, his gaze gleaming in the dark, riveted in a very strange way on my face.

— Do I have cake on my nose? I'm warning you, if that's the case and you let me take it across town, I'll never speak to you again!

He raised his hand and gently ran his thumb over my cheek, sowing even more doubt as to whether there was any food on my face, before finally replying:

— Shut up, you idiot.

The next moment, without warning, that face, so perfect and already so close, melted onto mine, covering my lips, still sweet from the honey biscuits I'd wolfed down, in an unpredictable kiss.

Not getting attached...

For all the time we'd been looking for each other, sometimes bickering, hanging around each other, it was bound to happen eventually... But I didn't know what his real aim was. Was he waiting for this? He wasn't the impulsive type... But the location suggested that he could just as easily give in to his primal instincts with no ulterior motive other than to use me for who I was. So there was nothing wrong with that, was there?

On the strength of this conviction, I pressed my lips against his, tacitly agreeing to continue this exchange in the way he no doubt already had in mind. He stepped back, however, looking at me in a very different way, as if hesitating, before moving back to my mouth with undisguised desire. His impatience did not deceive me, and very quickly our exchanges became even more spirited. His tongue took advantage of a sigh to meet mine in a breathless ballet. His powerful arms encircled my body, still showing a certain awkwardness when the skin of my bare back came into contact with his. He made me feel fragile, precious, and didn't rush his movements despite my pleas showing my growing desire. I liked his manners as much as he annoyed me, and, giving in to my own impulses, I slipped my hands under his top, determined to find out a little more about the mysterious man in front of me. And there was nothing that could disappoint me there, the marked furrows of his burning abs scrolling under my caresses, without surprise, when you saw her build that no tunic, no matter how loose, could sufficiently hide.

Carried away in this momentum, I felt him lift me effortlessly, his hands pressed under my thighs, simultaneously trying to open the still locked door of the building, no doubt wanting a little more privacy. His own impatience excited me as much as it amused me, and it was with a mischievous smile that I slowly took out the key from my cleavage, before waving it under his nose. He grabbed it unceremoniously, and I tightened my legs around his waist so as not to slip, while he opened, not without difficulty, the heavy door which stubbornly barred his way. With all this mess, it's lucky that everyone is already busy, or already in bed, leaving us the field free, without the slightest questioning!

He climbed the stairs he knew by heart, four by four, to my room, snatching a few stolen kisses from me along the way, and finally entered the room before slamming the door without further ceremony behind him. With that, my whole neighbourhood was warned: I would not sleep alone tonight!

I snickered at the thought, and he smiled back with that burning gaze still on, telling me that we were definitely having the exact same thing on our minds right now. I let myself be hypnotised, caressing his growing beard, so rough against my soft skin, taking the time to admire him a little, for once. Well, until he decided to take possession of my lips again, pressing my back against the cold wall next to the door, my behind resting in balance on what must have been my hall cabinet.

I then plunged my hands into his messy hair, always giving more depth to our languorous exchanges. Everything was becoming sulphurous between us so quickly, far from the long conversations we had had, as if we were finally letting our bodies speak after having held them back for so long. Was that what he had felt? And me ? I couldn't even remember if I had desired it before that. Desired... I gradually became aware of all these emotions he was provoking in me, but before I had time to analyse them, a moan escaped me as he took hold of one of my breasts. The firmness of his gesture contrasted with the softness of his thumb brushing my nipple through the fabric covering my chest, which was quick to react to his passage. He detached himself from our kiss, lowering his eyes to look without the slightest restraint at this bust that made more than one man's head spin, continuing his exploration with a feverish movement along the curve that my neckline easily let him see. I took the opportunity to slide my own hands under his top, pushing him to let go of me to swing over his head, and swing it away unceremoniously, so that I, too, could access all of his lovely merchandise. Faced with this divine spectacle that presented itself to me, I could only bite my lower lip, already learning it by heart from all possible senses, giving free rein to the incandescence of my lower abdomen, which demanded always more.

His gaze was amused to see me coveting him so much, but he too was asking for more fairness, and I felt my dress immediately fall from my shoulders, instantly revealing everything he had not yet had access to. The sight seemed to please him just as much, and his hands resumed their journey down my neck, sliding down the middle of my chest, down to my navel, in a gesture so gentle it seemed my skin was the more fragile thing than it has ever been given to possess. He leaned in the next moment, placing searing kisses from the base of my erect chest to its curves.

— Damn, Sati…" he growled, unable to hide his admiration, which would have made me lose my footing immediately, if I hadn't insisted on savouring every moment that was finally given to us.

To not get attached…

This sentence drummed in me at the same rhythm as my heart. It was the rule for all of us. We cannot suffer if we do not grant feelings to the other...

Amon

She was so beautiful, so... perfect. Her chest stood between us like a treasure, exhilaratingly beautiful, a piece of jewellery that she wore proudly, no longer waiting for me to take care of her. I wanted to take her and make her mine, right now. But I contained myself. She deserved far more consideration, and I just as much wanted these moments to last forever, etching each memory indelibly in my memory. Who knows if I could touch her again one day? And if everything changed between us, if she avoided me, this time, as she did with all these men who attached themselves a little too much to her.

Don't think, Amon, not now.

I let go of her voluptuous chest to go up to a point that had bothered me for a while. Lodged in his neck, several marks made me frown, and I intended to hide them with my own. She was mine tonight, and it was through her moans that I tried to make every hickey dropped by those disgusting beings at the festival disappear, until I got to the back of her neck, where a scorpion tattoo taunted me a little more. The mark of Shaa-em-uas, the man who had broken her, who had made her this woman who refused all feelings.

This man didn't deserve her any more than the others, it was all his fault. And yet it is, so to speak, thanks to him if Sati stretched out in my arms at this very moment. I let myself be devoured by my desire to possess her, forgetting even my old superstitions to even hear her voice vibrate once again. My hands roamed over her soft skin, and I finally grabbed her around the waist, pulling her to me unceremoniously this time. She immediately spread her thighs to let me pass, and I fit perfectly against her, leaving her plenty of time to perceive the desire that animated me between our still covered crotch. She didn't ignore it, I noticed it in her predatory gaze, as it followed my face, resuming my activities along her collarbones.

I kissed, then gently licked the marks of my competitors adorning the area, before repeatedly biting and sucking on her skin, so as to completely cover them with my own. The sighs that escaped between her lips drove me crazy, as did her fingernails scratching my back slightly when my gesture began to hurt her.

Satisfied to have regained my territory, I plunged on her lips again, finally giving in to the temptation that had become far too great to take care of her breasts hardened with pleasure. I kissed them in turn, teasing her nipples with my fingertips, or else with the tip of my expert tongue, biting them in turn, to hear her still sigh with relief. I had seen many other breasts, when I was still travelling on bloodthirsty missions, but hers was in my eyes no other like it, and I revelled in it as assiduously as envy, which was dangerously consuming me, allowed it.

Her knees tightened against my hips, like a call to go further, and I won't be asked, for a long time already far too cramped under my pants. I straightened up to make way for her, and it was trembling that she began to undo the last clothes that stood in her way.

Tonight, Sati, you will experience an intoxication of a completely different kind than the one I tried to free you from!

Sati

Never had a man pushed my desire to such an extent... They were usually reluctant to listen to my body, contenting themselves with satisfying their fantasies for me like simple beasts, and very rarely with the gentleness that Amon showed at that moment. He was nevertheless surprisingly possessive, and above all, treated my body as if it were a sacred temple. My senses were on full display, and I couldn't take it any longer before begging for a little more myself.

I pushed him back slightly, climbing down from the chest of drawers where he had perched me, and let his pants slip, along with my dress, at our feet. I stood naked in front of him, convinced to take the upper hand when he had one last piece of underwear left to resist me. In my turn, I ran through his chest bubbling with delicate kisses, taking care, going down lower and lower, to let my chest brush against his stretched member under this last fabric. I taunted him, and it was with satisfaction that I heard him growl at this contact. I then took the opportunity to put a hickey on his hip.

— Sati...

He was already saying my name, with that raspy and terribly sexy voice, but I was just getting started, sweetie~.

I responded to his call, torturing him a little more by letting his member slide more frankly between my breasts, tearing him a new rattle without the slightest difficulty. If he must have known women in his life, was it the same for the practices taught to us by the matriarchs of the place? I gloated inwardly to push him to his limits, swearing to myself to make him lose his mind. Amon Donkor, tonight you will be all mine!

He suddenly grabbed part of my hair, pulling it back in the hope of making me let go, but I certainly wasn't done with him! And it was with unmasked greed that I freed the object of my desires from its prison of fabric, letting this last rampart invariably join his pants on the ground.

— Sati… You're not ob — …

He guessed what I was planning to do, and not wanting to let his politeness interfere with my plan, I looked up at him before executing, not missing a beat of each of his reactions to come. I caressed his bump with one hand, the veins throbbing with the pleasure I gave him. His breathing became shorter, almost jerky, scraping the back of his now dry throat. A smirk, and I inserted his only known weak spot into my eager mouth, deftly playing my tongue as he grew inside me. He tugged at my hair once more, in a sudden surge of pleasure, before finally giving in and urging me on, deeper and harder each time.

Amon

Damn, this girl was driving me crazy! I used to dominate the situation, but now I was no longer in control, finding myself at the mercy of his evil mouth. As I felt myself coming, I finally lifted her by force, not wanting to finish already, and especially not alone. She let go of the object of her lust before the fatal moment, breathless, a victorious smile on her lips, while I tried to regain my senses. But I cut her off from her hopes immediately.

— It's only just begun, Sati.

The glint that followed in her eyes confirmed that the message had got through. I grabbed her with a firm hand, bringing her back against me to kiss her again, playing with this devil's tongue that would have almost got the better of me. We were now in the simplest device, and I always found her more beautiful, more desirable ... Feelings that I found flattering in her hungry pupils.

I took her chin gently, lifting her face to mine so she could read all the desire I felt for her, and she put her arms around my neck, as if to tell me that she really wanted to, her too. I then let my hand creep into her sensitive area, the last treasure I had yet to taste. I caressed her gently as she began to kiss again. But it didn't take long before she pulled away, no doubt already warmed up by her previous ruse, and let out in a pleading breath, like a signal:

— Amon…

This name, my beauty, I want to hear you scream it.
I let go of her intimacy to take it back under her thighs, strongly leaning against a wall by making her let out a new moan. Her pelvis rubbing against mine, I let her find the ideal position for her, and it was she who launched the first assault, fearless, slowly, her arms around my neck, while my rattle accompanied her sigh to finally feel its damp walls on my erect manhood.

Without further ado, I began to move my pelvis, more and more lively, more and more strong, stimulated by the slapping of her skin against mine, and even more by the moans that she contained with difficulty.

I bit her neck, in a warning, and whispered to her:

— I want to hear you, Sati.

She bit my lip back, in a fit of revenge, before gazing darkly into mine, unleashing the pleasure I was giving her with each of my unrestrained assaults.

If you knew how crazy I am about you...

Her voice pushed me beyond my limits, singing its sweet high notes. I wanted more, always more. Her nails scratched the back of my neck, her body tense between my hands, she couldn't take it anymore, I could see it, but I couldn't let myself go with her, not yet. And what I wanted more than anything was not long in coming:

— Amon...ah...

Her voice grew louder, beyond her control, repeating my name in an orgasm I now shared with her. A final thrust, and I too freed myself, moaning against her neck, under the tension of brutal pleasure. How to explain what had just happened? I was panting, disconnected from this reality that I was struggling to realise. Did she really feel the same? I couldn't bring myself to be just another name on her list… I wanted to be different from the others, I wanted to introduce her to unknown sensations, it was a great pretension, when one knew what kind of clientele struggled to get a night of grace...

I caught my breath, slowly, my body hot and wet against hers, before setting her back, staggering, against the wall.

It was so perfect, so intense that time could well have stopped there, I had nothing more to do, persuaded never to experience such a moment again. I tucked one of her locks of hair behind her ear, clearing her flushed face from the effort, and making sure she was okay at the same time. Her smile, huge and sincere, is enough to reassure me. I didn't know what would happen after that, but this suspended time seemed to work for both of us. We were one, like it was the most natural thing in the world, like it was all inevitable, after all the arguing and bickering. I didn't even know how we got here.

She tried to take a step, shaking, and I caught her, fearing she might collapse. She pointed to a door, and I carried her like a princess to the indicated place. The bathroom, of course. We both needed to get our wits together, and I was naive to think that a shower was the best idea. I entered with her, and began to wet a towel to help her. She took the cloth, but instead of using it for herself, she began to pass it over my body. I was pretty sure that she didn't reserve this kind of treatment for all of her "guests".

You're looking for trouble, Sati...

I watched her, removing her hair from her finery. She had nothing on her, no more jewellery or finery, and she was softer and more natural than I had seen her, and I liked that. In a surge of modesty at my insistent gaze, she turned her back on me, unconsciously letting me see what I was still unaware of until then. My eyes inevitably slid along the descent of her loins, stopping on her posterior calling for indecency.

Damn she was beautiful...

I grabbed her by the hips, crossing my hands under her stomach to pull her closer to me. She turned her face slightly towards me, realising that this gentle gesture was not innocent.

You will drive me crazy...

I could hardly hide my desire, beating in this comfortable furrow that had presented itself to me. With an undulation of the hip that immediately made me lose the little reason I had left, she made me understand that she wanted it just as much, too, and I did not need to be asked a second time.

The humidity of the room welcomed the muffled sounds of our antics. She was mine once again, and I could have possessed her for hours on end, kissing every inch of her skin and memorising every sound her mouth made, all the better to satisfy her.

But something was off this time. A new orgasm that awakened in her what she had been trying to hide for several years now. As she turned around, shaking with both pleasure and dread, I caught sight of the cause of that dark aura I could feel from the deathblow, slowly crossing her face. Her gaze had changed, her features had drawn, and the tattooed scorpion on her neck now seemed to extend to her shoulder.

The mark of Shaa-em-uas... Thebes' most famous healer, now accused and wanted for sorcery across the land. So the rumours were true. But I didn't have time to worry about this blatant proof of his guilt, when mine had just caused Sati to lose control.

— Sati...

I hugged her close, protectively, trying to calm her down as I saw her pain growing in her eyes.

Shit... I shouldn't have pushed her that far...

— Sati, I'm here.

I looked at her, caressing her cheek in a soothing gesture, assuring her of my presence at her side. I would never leave her, and I repeated to her in this same promise that her secret would never come out of these walls. If they learned that she had been touched by her master's witchcraft, they would surely execute her before sunrise... And that was not something I could tolerate. Shaa-em-uas had already hurt her enough, he wouldn't take her life anymore!

It took her long minutes to stabilise, and finally see her mark return to its original place, leaving her exhausted in my arms. She had never wanted to tell me about her life before she arrived in Thebes, or what this scorpion meant to her. But I understood. I also understood that she kept this burden as a memory of what she had felt for him, perhaps in the hope of one day seeing him again, just as I kept my stories for the sole purpose of redeeming myself in waiting to find them...

Her breathing calmed down as well, and I wrapped her in a towel to help her out. She no longer uttered a word, but I knew the rest of the procedure.

No attachment.

So I put her gently in her bed, making sure one last time that she was well enough, and got up to leave her apartment. It was like that, for me, as for her, we didn't sleep with our conquests, we slept, and we left. No goodbye, and especially no reunion. I would only remember what we had shared. Would I regret the hours spent by her side? The future would tell me soon enough.

But my heart leaps then, at this contact that I dared not hope for. Her hand in mine, she timidly pulled me in, silently requesting my presence at her side. This time it was different, we wouldn't leave each other... Not right away.

I gave in without flinching, I had become addicted, and even if I blamed myself for hoping that, maybe it was time for us to relearn how to live...

Sati

He lay down next to me, and I slipped into his strong and comforting arms. I was still shaken by what had happened, it was true, but that wasn't really why I wanted him to stay.

I couldn't confess to him, but what I really wanted was for him to come back to this bed every night from today on... He now knew my secret, and hadn't left to denounce me. He was there... He had always been there. I felt so stupid for finally letting my heart give in, even more so for this man who didn't care about feelings, just like me...

But, as if reading my thoughts, he did what I hadn't expected, in a whisper so delicate that I barely heard him:

— I love you.